D1108429
Gambier
Is.
•Vancouver
Bowen Is.
Keats Is.
SALISH SEA
Saturna Is.
Mayne
Is.
Galiano Is.
Gabriola Is.
Valdes Is.
Entrance Is.
Jedediah Is.
N
S
Prevost Is.
Pender
Islands
Thetis Is.
Salt Spring Is.
Penelakut Is.
DeCourcy Is.
D'Arcy Is.
VANCOUVER ISLAND
Victoria
Discovery Is.

GULF ISLANDS ALPHABET

I dedicate this book to my Lasqueti Island-born daughter, Similkameen. You bring me such joy, while continuously surprising and inspiring me. I love you with all my heart! And to Paddy, for helping make all my island dreams come true! You are my rock. I love, respect and admire you!

- Love Mum/Bronwyn

To my parents, Linda and Bill, thank you for your continuous support over the years. Your critical eyes and continuous suggestions have been invaluable in making me a better artist as well as a person.

- Alex

Published in 2011 by Simply Read Books www.simplyreadbooks.com

Library and Archives Canada Cataloguing in Publication

Preece, Bronwyn, 1978-
Gulf Islands alphabet / Bronwyn Preece ; Alex Walton, illustrator.

ISBN 978-1-897476-29-1 HC
ISBN 978-1-897476-86-4 PB

1. English language--Alphabet--Juvenile literature. 2. Gulf Islands (B.C.)--Pictorial works--Juvenile literature. 3. Alphabet books.
I. Walton, Alex II. Title.

PE1155.P73 2010 j421'.1 C2009-904062-X

We gratefully acknowledge for their financial support of our publishing program the Canada Council for the Arts, the BC Arts Council, and the Government of Canada through the Canada Book Fund (CBF).

Manufactured by Hung Hing in China, March 2011
This product conforms to CPSIA 2008

Book design by Natasha Kanji

10 9 8 7 6 5 4 3 2 1

GULF ISLANDS ALPHABET

Bronwyn Preece ~ Illustrated by Alex Walton

SIMPLY READ BOOKS

Out of British Columbia's southwestern waters of the Salish Sea, known also as the Strait of Georgia, rises the Gulf Islands archipelago. The more than four hundred and fifty islands and islets are remarkable for their Mediterranean-like climate: warm, dry summers and mild, wet winters. As part of the coastal Douglas-fir ecosystem, these islands support spectacular western red cedars and exotic-looking Arbutus trees. The area is also home to one of the last vestiges of the Garry oak ecosystem, which is listed as one of Canada's most at-risk habitats.

The Gulf Islands are Salish First Nations' traditional territory. Europeans began settling the area in the 1800s, and many local place names reflect this history. In recognition of the unique land and sensitive features of the Gulf Islands, the Islands Trust, a special level of local government, was established by the provincial government in 1974 to manage land use decisions. The Trust is guided by a mandate to preserve and protect the area. In 2003, the federal government created the Gulf Islands National Park Reserve to protect part of the region. Today, the Gulf Islands are home to a diverse population of approximately twenty-five thousand permanent residents. Many more tourists than that visit the archipelago every year.

Around,

Amongst

And Amidst the Gulf Islands of

Amazing British Columbia, we …

Arrive through Active Pass, sighting

Anchors being set by sailors,

As we Admire

Arbutus trees

And Anemones Along …

Beaches

Bathed in a Bevy of

Brambles and Berries,

Bracken and Balsam.

Beyond,

Boats Bask in

Bays around

Bowen Island.

Beside a Bluff, hikers …

Clamber down a

Cliff to a

Cabin,

Cradled in a Cove on

Cortes Island,

Crowned by a Colossal

Cedar.

Driftwood below a

Denman Island

Dock waits to be scavenged, while

Day Dawns over the islands of

DeCourcy,

Discovery and

D'Arcy.

Eagles fly over

Estuaries,

Eventually landing on

Entrance Island.

Exploring these isles

Enchants us and others, who arrive on …

Ferries to

Fulford Harbour and

False Bay and boats that

Frequent

Fiddler's Cove.

Gorgeous Galleries on

Gabriola are

Guaranteed to be worth a Gander, and

Gallivanting on Galiano or Gambier is

Great fun, as is a

Gallop on over to

Gillies Bay or Going to Ganges for the day.

Hiking by Huckleberries and

Heritage Homesteads on

Hornby Island we see

Herons in flight,

Heading towards

Hope Bay and other

Hideaway Havens on …

Isolated Islets, where

Islanders

Introduce us to

Interesting sites Inviting further

Investigation.

Jaunts to
Jedediah,
Jelina and
Jervis Islands make for
Joyful Journeys.
Jellyfish swim in the ocean beneath …

K*ayaks and Kelp around Keats.*

Kingfishers cry as they fly towards …

Lakes and Lagoons, from

Lyall Harbour to

Lasqueti.

Legends and Lore are based on the

Lamps of Lighthouses serving as …

Markers for Mariners sailing from the

Mainland to Mayne Island, from

Manson's Landing down to Cape Mudge.

Maneuvering past

Mountains of Mussels, boats

Make their way through …

Narrows, where surging seas are

Notoriously difficult to

Nimbly Navigate.

Ocean waters around these islands are home to

Orcas and Octopi,

Oysters and Otters.

Overhead, an Osprey flies in …

Patterns Past the island of Penelakut.

Pender Island Poets compose

Pictorial Passages about this

Pacific Paradise, as they

Peer over Port Washington at

Prevost Island.

Quadra Island is

Quintessentially

Quaint and Quirky, where people follow …

Rambling Roads made

Rugged with Ruts from

Repeated Rain where a

Ragtag bunch of

Rascally Raccoons and

Raucous Ravens

Raise a Ruckus.

Setting Sail through the
Salish Sea, we leave the
Shores of Savary,
Sauntering Southward to
Saturna's Shoals of Starfish and
Salt Spring Island all
Speckled in Sheep, where we hope to
Spot the Seldom-Seen
Sharp-tailed Snake.

Turning Towards
Thetis, we

Tack Through
The Tug of
The Tide.

Time is set in
Telegraph Harbour
To leave for
Texada Island.

Umbrellas
Unfurl, as rain
Unleashes
Upon Us.

Vessels

Voyage between

Victoria and

Vancouver, while we Visit with other

Vacationers

Venturing through

Virgin forests on

Valdes Island.

Wave and Whale Watching are

Wonderful activities of this

West Coast World,

Where We learn about …

Xeel's, the creator, in legends of the Hul'qumi'num people of the Salish Gulf Islands.

Yonder,

Yanked from its mooring in a storm, a

Yacht lies wrecked on the rocks off

Yeo Point.

Zooming about in our

Zodiac, we catch the wind's lingering

Zephyrs, as we

Zip , Zoot and

Zag between all the spectacular Gulf Islands of the Salish Sea.

BRITISH COLUMBIA'S MAINLAND